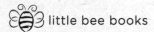 little bee books

251 Park Avenue South, New York, NY 10010
Copyright © 2019 by Little Bee Books
All rights reserved, including the right of reproduction in whole or in part in any form.
Library of Congress Cataloging-in-Publication Data is available upon request.
Manufactured in China   TPL 0819
ISBN 978-1-4998-0849-0 (PBK)
First Edition 10 9 8 7 6 5 4 3 2 1
ISBN 978-1-4998-0850-6 (HC)
First Edition 10 9 8 7 6 5 4 3 2 1

littlebeebooks.com

Mighty
BOOK 4
Meg

and the Super Disguise

BY
Sammy
Griffin

illustrated
BY
Micah
Player

Contents

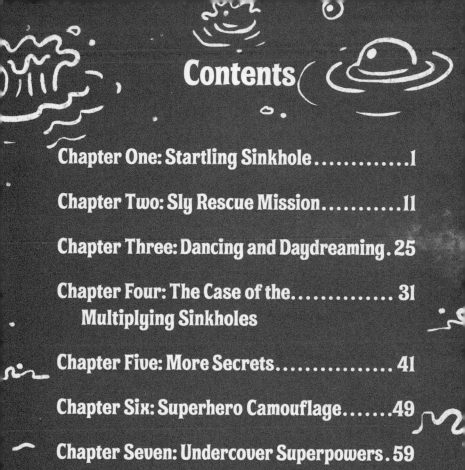

Chapter One:
Startling Sinkhole

The sun pricked at Meg's bare shoulders as she walked home from school with her little brother, Curtis. As they passed an empty field, the breeze picked up a voice crying and carried it to Meg's superpowered ears.

She looked at Curtis, who continued to skip over the sidewalk lines. The superpowers she got from her magic ring were hard at work again, and she needed to figure out what they were trying to tell her. Meg had to follow the sound.

She hurried, calling out to Curtis, who lagged behind. "Come on, C.! Let's check out the park."

Meg could now tell that the cry came from a mom calling to her child somewhere around the small playground two blocks outside Meg and Curtis's usual path to school. Turning down the street, Meg rushed Curtis along as they neared the park. A swing set and slide stood in a circle of dark playground bark. It was empty.

A tall mom with long hair frantically searched the parking lot of the apartment complex next door. "Caroline! Caroline!" she yelled. She ran between the parked cars, and dropped to her knees to search beneath them. Even without her super-hearing, Meg could tell that the mom's voice was starting to give.

"We should help her look," Curtis said.

Meg nodded just as another sound reached her. A whoosh echoed in her ears, followed by a gasp and a small cry. Her head snapped to where the noise came from, opposite the parking lot. A small, wooded area lined the back side of the playground.

"You help the mom look," Meg said. "I'm going to double-check the field."

"But it was empty," Curtis complained.

"I'll come right back," Meg promised, feeling her brother's eyes on her as she ran toward the slide. When Curtis's calls joined the mother's, Meg jetted toward the trees behind the park using her super-speed.

The woods were shadowy and crowded with tall pine trees that climbed up and over a small peak. Meg kicked against the thick brush underfoot as she ran, the twigs and pine needles scratching her skin. She stopped running and stood quietly, listening for more sounds. Another cry ahead pulled her forward, and when she reached the top of a hill, she nearly tumbled into a giant hole in the ground.

She peered inside,
but the hole was dark,
crowded with roots and
branches of broken trees.

8

"Help," a weak voice called from below. When Meg's eyes adjusted to the darkness, she saw a small girl cradled in between two tree trunks.

Chapter Two:
Sly Rescue Mission

As Meg brainstormed ways to rescue the girl from the sinkhole, she could hear Curtis and Caroline's mother draw closer. She had to figure out how to get Caroline out of the hole fast.

If Meg dropped to Caroline's perch, her weight might push the trees farther down the hole. Plus, Meg had to somehow pull Caroline free without revealing her own identity. She knew that once people discovered what she could do, someone was sure to take away the magic ring that had granted her superpowers.

12

Meg found a long, loose tree root dropping down the edge of the hole. It was as thick as her arm and looked like a giant worm. She knew how she would save the girl now! Closing her eyes for a deep, focused breath, Meg imagined herself disappearing. When she opened her eyes, her body had vanished. Lately, Meg had been working very hard to control her invisibility, and it looked like her recent superpower practice was finally paying off!

Meg took another deep breath, and when she exhaled, she backed away from the sturdy forest floor and jumped into the dark sinkhole.

Meg waved her arms in front of her, grabbing for the tree root and letting it slide through her hands until she was just above the girl. Her fingers clamped down on the rubbery wood, and she swung 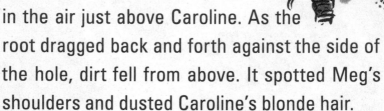 in the air just above Caroline. As the root dragged back and forth against the side of the hole, dirt fell from above. It spotted Meg's shoulders and dusted Caroline's blonde hair.

15

Meg stared at her dirty arms, the soil covering her clothes. She could see herself again! Try as she might to imagine herself invisible, all her superpowers seemed to be channeled into her super-strength. Caroline huddled below, ducking her head as the dirt continued to sprinkle down. Meg would have to figure out another way to make sure Caroline didn't see her.

Meg reached down, wrapping one arm around the little girl's waist while clutching the root with the other. Caroline yelped in surprise, but then she relaxed against Meg.

Somehow Meg needed to escape the sinkhole while holding Caroline. Meg dropped onto Caroline's perch, and with all her strength, she leapt up, launching them toward the hole's opening as the tree trunk collapsed into the pit beneath them.

Still holding Caroline from behind, Meg set her gently onto the ground. Before the girl had a chance to look around, Meg jumped as far from her and the sinkhole as possible, landing in a cluster of trees bordering the park. She listened closely as Curtis and Caroline's mother continued to call for the girl. They sounded like they were almost to the top of the hill.

Using her super-speed, Meg raced back toward Curtis and Caroline's mother, slowing down when she saw them crest the hill. Putting on her most convincing expression of surprise, Meg ran toward Curtis, meeting him at the sinkhole.

Caroline cried in her mother's arms, trying to explain that she had been in the hole one minute and then yanked from it the next. Caroline could've sworn someone saved her, but when she was outside the hole, she was all alone. Meg enjoyed the feeling of relief that spread across her body like goose bumps. The girl was safe, and so was her secret.

"Thank you so much for your help," Caroline's mom told Curtis, who smiled shyly.

But when her brother looked up at Meg, his eyes cut into a suspicious glare. "Why are you so dirty?" he asked her.

Meg looked down, causing dust to fall from her head. She brushed the dirt from her arms and answered. "I fell down the hill when I was trying to catch up to you."

Curtis chuckled. "You're such a klutz," he said.

Meg chucked him on the shoulder. "We should go home before Latisha starts to worry about us." Their babysitter would call Mom if they didn't make it home on time.

As they walked home, Curtis talked nonstop about the sinkhole. While he talked, Meg realized that even though she had managed to save Caroline without being caught, she still needed some kind of plan for using her superpowers in public. Meg needed a disguise.

Chapter Three:
Dancing and Daydreaming

During recess the next day, Meg, Ruby, and Tara practiced their new dance routine. The girls swung their hips to a song Ruby had made up, stopping on the eighth count to throw out their arms and jump as high as they could. Meg was careful not to jump too high. They strutted backward a few steps before spinning to face the opposite direction, taking turns doing high kicks.

A small group of second graders had gathered to watch them, oohing and aahing as the friends moved in sync. Jackson had stopped behind their admirers to glare at Meg before his friend Porter called him over to play tetherball. He lasered Meg with one last scowl and then jogged away.

"From the top," Tara cried out, and the three girls took their places again. Ruby yelled out a quick countdown and started to sing, the girls stepping through their routine almost as naturally as breathing.

As they danced, Meg thought about the close call with Caroline yesterday, and how Curtis and the girl's mother could have crested the hill just as Meg leapt from the sinkhole with Caroline in her arms. They both would have known that no ordinary girl could save someone from a gaping hole in the ground like that.

Using her superpowers in public put her at risk of being discovered. But Meg had to use her abilities to help people, and that meant that sometimes others would see her. She needed a costume or a disguise to prevent that from happening.

Meg laughed out loud as she imagined herself in a cape and mask. Tara and Ruby eyed her as they spun to the ending of their routine, and Meg covered her mouth to stifle more giggles.

After they relaxed their jazz hands, the small audience asked if the girls could teach them the routine, and Meg, Ruby, and Tara grinned at the idea.

The girls walked through their steps slowly this time, and while they did, Meg decided that a simple disguise would be much better than a full costume. She just needed to keep her real identity a secret, and a disguise would help her accomplish just that.

Their new students laughed as they matched the girls' movements, and Meg forgot all about her superpowers as she enjoyed a fun, ordinary recess.

Chapter Four:
The Case of the
Multiplying Sinkholes

On the way to Ruby's house after school, the girls caught a glimpse of the park Caroline had wandered away from the day before. Two big city trucks had pulled onto the grass surrounding the playground.

"What's going on over there?" Ruby asked.

"That's where Curtis and I found the girl who fell into the sinkhole," Meg said. "It was ginormous, like a bottomless pit."

"Let's go check it out!" Tara yelled as she darted ahead of her friends without waiting for them to answer.

Meg and Ruby followed after her, their shoes slapping on the pavement. Like the day before, the playground was empty.

"Where's the sinkhole?" Tara whispered, even though there was no one else nearby to hear her.

Meg pointed past the trees. "Over there!"

The girls slowly made their way into the woods, Meg leading them toward the sound of people talking. As they neared the top of the hill, the girls crouched behind a thick pine so they wouldn't be shooed away by the adults.

The three workers were standing around the dark sinkhole. They peered over the edge cautiously, as if a mud monster might leap out at them.

The tallest of the three workers said, "We'll pour a layer of cement, fill the hole with sand, and then top it off with some dirt." They all nodded, agreeing with the plan.

As they backed away from the hole, a fierce groan echoed behind them. The girls watched in horror as a patch of trees was swallowed by the earth, dropping out of view and into the ground. The workers hollered in surprise and sprinted away from the spot, stopping just shy of the girls' hiding place.

"What was that?" one of the men asked.

"Another sinkhole," the woman responded. And then she added, in a whisper, "What is going *on* out here?"

Meg was thinking the same thing. She remembered the strange river that had formed out of nowhere, nearly drowning her neighbor's dog, Max. And then there were the ice formations that appeared by her school on a warm spring day. Now, Plainview had these scary sinkholes. It seemed that ever since Meg had gotten her magic ring, unusual things had begun happening around her town, and each one was more dangerous than the last.

Chapter Five:
More Secrets

The girls spent another recess dancing on the playground. After the bell, they walked back toward the school building, all of them out of breath. Ruby and Tara chatted excitedly about creating a new routine.

Ruby, pink-cheeked and smiling, said, "I know Curtis doesn't have Homework Club today, but why don't you come over after school so we can practice?"

41

Meg groaned. "Sorry, guys. Latisha's expecting us." Even though she knew her babysitter probably wouldn't mind the break, Meg had planned to work on her disguise after school and didn't want to put it off.

Tara stopped outside the school doors, jutted out a hip, and frowned. "Really? Even if your mom gives you permission?"

Tara pushed ahead of Ruby and Meg as the three girls stumbled into the hallway, which echoed with laughter and crowded conversations.

Meg said, "She wouldn't want to trouble Ruby's mom any extra."

"It's no trouble," Ruby insisted, pulling on Meg's arm. "Come on, Meggers! We could practice for the school talent show—it'd be so much fun!"

Meg hated avoiding her friends like this, especially when it required a little dishonesty, but until she could fully control her invisibility with her other superpowers, she needed a disguise. "Sorry, guys. Mom has a super-important meeting this afternoon, and I'm not allowed to interrupt unless it's a real emergency. But we can totally get started tomorrow." And there was the white lie— Mom hadn't told Meg about any important meetings today.

Tara grumbled under her breath and Ruby rolled her eyes as the girls walked into science class.

This wasn't the first time Meg had lied to her friends because of her magic ring. When she first discovered the superpowers it gave her, she had avoided them for a week in order to practice her new skills.

The girls sat at their desks, a triangle of seats with Tara in back and Meg and Ruby in front of her. They twisted in their chairs, out of habit, ready to chat until class started. But since they were disappointed that Meg wouldn't be coming over after school, the girls shrugged sadly and looked away.

Guilt pressed on Meg's chest, making her heart achy. She hated keeping secrets from her best friends. Would she have to hide her superpowers from them forever? The thought of keeping a never-ending secret made Meg tired and grouchy. She trusted Ruby and Tara more than almost anyone else in the world. Surely, she'd be able to share her secret with them someday.

Chapter Six:
Superhero Camouflage

Meg lay down on her bedroom floor, a notebook in front of her and the dress-up bin by her side.

She had been doing a lot of thinking
about superheroes and how they disguise
their identities to protect themselves and
those they love. Most of them wore full-
body costumes, some with capes, some with
masks, and some with both.

Meg opened the notebook, tapping a pencil on the blank page. While costumes may have worked for superheroes in movies, they weren't possible in real life. She imagined changing into a full costume before jumping into the sinkhole to rescue Caroline. The little girl would have fallen to the bottom of the pit before Meg could have disguised herself. Besides, where would she carry a costume like that? And how would she change without anyone seeing her?

Meg wrote some notes on the page. Whatever disguise she used would need to be small enough to carry around with her, smaller even than a backpack. She remembered the fanny pack she had bought with her birthday money last summer.

She stood and walked to her dresser, rummaging through the second drawer, where she kept her socks, pajamas, and a handful of treasures. There, tucked in  the back corner next to a prism Aunt Nikki had given her and a locket from Grandma Buckland, was the blue-and-yellow, reversible fanny pack that clasped around her waist. She tried it on, adjusting the strap so it fit snugly.

SNAP!

This was great! As long as her disguise fit into this pouch, Meg could carry it with her everywhere.

She went back to her spot on the floor and began digging through the dress-up bin to find things that would fit inside the pack.

She made a small pile of items: false crooked teeth, a curly orange wig, sunglasses, an enormous pink bow tie, a red-and-gold head scarf, and a visor with fake brown hair frizzing up at the top. Meg examined the items, placing pieces together to see what she thought of the different combinations.

Smiling at her final selection, she stuffed her new disguise into her fanny pack and buckled it across her body like a sash. Meg stood in front of the mirror behind her closed door. Testing to see how quickly she could put it on, she unzipped the fanny pack, wrapped the red-and-gold head scarf over her hair, and slipped on the sunglasses.

Meg posed for herself, hands on hips, and turned to see how she looked from the side. Perfect!

Chapter Seven:
Undercover Superpowers

$\mathcal{M}$eg was supposed to meet Ruby and Tara at the sinkhole park on Saturday so the girls could examine the filled holes. But Meg was so excited to try out her new disguise that she left thirty minutes early to see if there might be a chance for her to use it.

Meg's mom agreed to let her go alone, even though Curtis had begged to go, too. Mom understood the importance of good old-fashioned girl time and warned her to call if they ended up going to Tara's or Ruby's house instead.

Patting her fanny pack as she hit the sidewalk, Meg skipped to the park, happy that her mom and Curtis hadn't questioned her new accessory. So far, so good.

A handful of little kids roamed the playground, their moms watching from nearby benches. Meg walked around them and into the woods, stopping when she reached the small clearings where the sinkholes used to be. Both holes had been filled in, marked on top by mounds of dark earth. Meg tentatively stepped onto one of the circles with her sneaker, testing to make sure it was steady. She stayed aboveground.

As Meg searched the area for new sinkholes, she heard yelling from the other side of the trees. Following this new noise, she came to the end of the woods where it opened into a small, sandy field.

Watching from behind a thick tree, Meg spotted four boys trying to pull their friend out of the ground. Meg rubbed at her eyes, not sure what she was seeing. The boy seemed to have been swallowed by the sand! Everything below his waist was somehow stuck underground. And he was sinking.

It was quicksand, Meg realized. The boy was stuck in quicksand!

Her heart flapped around in her chest like a startled bird. This was her chance!

Meg unzipped her fanny pack and put on her disguise, her fingers trembling a bit as she tied the head scarf. She brushed down her shirt before stepping from the trees and approaching the boys.

"Can I help?" Meg asked. All the boys turned to look at her, even the one stuck in the ground. Some of them were her age, and she even knew a few from her classes at school.

Despite the seriousness of the situation, they studied Meg, their dazed expressions passing from her scarf to her sunglasses to her fanny pack and back again.

"Who are you?" Tom, a lanky kid from her math class, asked. Meg adjusted her scarf a bit and hoped he wouldn't recognize her.

"A friend," Meg answered. And then, to force them from their quiet stupor, she quickly added, "We don't have a lot of time. Let's get to work."

66

Chapter Eight: Outwitting Quicksand

The boys turned back to their friend, yanking on his arm and trying to jostle him free. Meg watched in horror as their efforts seemed to be making him sink even deeper.

"STOP!" she yelled. They turned to look at her again, and she explained, "It's not helping. He's getting more stuck."

"So what do we do?" Tom asked.

"Let me think," she said, rewinding through all the science lessons Mr. Fester had taught her class about natural phenomenon. He had talked a little about quicksand, explaining that the most natural human response to it was not the most helpful. You had to relax and avoid panic.

"What's your name?" Meg asked the boy.

"Ethan," he whimpered. The quicksand had reached his chest, and the tears in his eyes threatened to spill onto his cheeks.

"Hi, Ethan." Meg squatted down to look him in the eyes as they talked. "Take deep breaths and float on your back, like you do in the water. That way you won't sink."

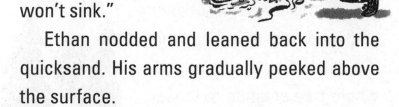

Ethan nodded and leaned back into the quicksand. His arms gradually peeked above the surface.

"Now," Meg said, "slowly wiggle your legs free. I'll grab a branch to help get you out."

Meg studied the trees. She super-jumped into the air and accidentally sailed high over a pine tree. She wasn't used to having an audience. On her way down, she grabbed one of the thicker branches and tried to pull it free from the trunk. For a second, the whole tree seemed to loosen in the ground. Meg was afraid

she would pop the entire thing from the earth. But then the branch snapped away, and she dropped back down. The ground shook a bit as she landed.

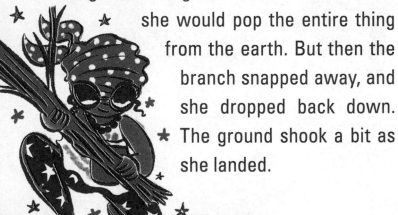

The branch was taller than Meg and would cover the quicksand perfectly. She jogged back to the group, carrying the branch under one arm.

Ethan's friends continued to watch Meg like she was a unicorn or a yeti, but she didn't have time to worry about them.

Ethan's legs rose to the surface, his knees sticking out from the quicksand. It almost looked like he was making a sand angel.

Meg dropped the branch lengthwise next to Ethan so it lay over the patch of quicksand like a small bridge. If he rolled onto the branch, he would be on more stable ground.

"Ethan," Meg said. "Can you roll over the branch to the other side?"

Ethan nodded. He pulled one arm free from the quicksand and threw it over the branch. The movement made his body turn toward Meg's bridge, and the group watched as he straddled the branch and then rolled over it and onto solid ground. His friends surrounded him, cheering. And then, just to be safe, they dragged him even farther from the quicksand.

Chapter Nine:
Caught in a Costume

It took a few minutes, but Ethan finally stood up, his body covered in sandy sludge.

He faced Meg. "Thank you for helping." His friends mumbled their thanks too, still looking dazed by the whole experience.

"We should get out of here," one of them said, and the rest nodded.

Tom pulled Ethan's arm around his shoulder and helped him catch up with the group. Meg watched the boys as they limped away. They had just passed by two familiar figures who stood gaping at the edge of the woods, their mouths hanging open in the shape of capital Os.

It was Tara and Ruby.

"Meg?" Ruby asked.

Oh no, Meg thought. Her friends must have wandered into the woods when Meg didn't show up on time to meet them at the park. *How much did they see?*

She realized they were standing only ten yards away from where she had just broken the branch using her super-strength. Maybe she could convince them that she was someone else.

Clearing her throat, she tried responding in a deep voice. "Who's Meg?"

Tara crossed her arms over her chest and glared at Meg. "Seriously? We've been best friends for two years, and you're going to try to fool me?"

Meg shook her head. These were her best friends, and she couldn't keep this from them anymore. She pulled the glasses off her face and the head scarf from her head. "Hi?"

Ruby and Tara looked at each other and then back at Meg. All at once they rattled off so many questions, talking over one another and making no sense. Meg shook her head in confusion, and they stopped.

Ruby nodded at Tara, and Tara went first.
"How did you jump so high into that tree and
break that huge branch?"

Meg took a deep breath, held it for a few seconds, and then released it in one big blow. "Remember that ring Aunt Nikki gave me for my birthday?" Her friends nodded. "It gives me superpowers."

Tara scoffed. "What?"

Meg nodded, and the two girls eyed her suspiciously. "Okay. Watch," she said. Meg jumped high into the air, shooting out of sight for a few seconds before barreling back to the ground, landing in a crouch.

Then, concentrating for a second, Meg disappeared, walked closer to her friends, and reappeared right in front of them. This time, their mouths were wide open, their eyes glazed over in shock.

"So those tricks you did for our mini-Olympics, and the time you jumped onto the fence to save Dan. . . ." Tara trailed off as she thought back. "And nearly knocking over that marble column at Ruby's house?"

"Superpowers," Meg confirmed.

Chapter Ten:
No More Secrets

The girls had become so quiet that Meg didn't know what to do. She sat down on a rock and waited for them to respond.

"Why didn't you tell us?" Ruby muttered so quietly that Meg had to use her super-hearing to understand.

Her best friends leaned so close to one another that their shoulders touched. Meg could tell that keeping this secret had hurt their feelings.

Meg stood up. "I'm sorry. I was afraid someone would take away the ring if anyone found out."

"We wouldn't do that," Ruby said matter-of-factly. "We're best friends."

Meg smiled. "I know. You're right," she said. "I should have told you. It was wrong to keep this a secret from my besties."

"Let's all pinkie-promise never to keep all secrets from each other." Tara held her fist toward Ruby and Meg, her pinkie sticking out.

The girls giggled as they linked pinkies.

"And," Meg said, "let's also promise never to tell anyone about my superpowers. I trust you two, but the more people that know, the harder it will be to keep this a secret!"

They each promised never to tell anyone about Meg's superpowers.

"Can we be your partners?" Ruby asked as they made their way back through the woods and toward the park. "Or maybe your superhero managers?"

Meg laughed. "Of course." Then she thought about the quicksand and the sinkholes. She had to tell them one more thing. "Since I got the ring, all these weird things have been happening in Plainview—like the sinkholes and the quicksand. I need to find out if they're somehow connected to my superpowers."

"We'll help!" Tara said, and Ruby nodded. "But just one thing."

The girls reached the park and stopped walking. "What?" Meg asked.

"You probably shouldn't wear that silly disguise anymore," Tara said. "It's a little distracting. You'll get more attention wearing it than you would just being you."

"Yeah," Ruby agreed. "You looked like a fortune-teller. It's kind of ridiculous."

The three girls busted into sidesplitting laughter, Meg hooting louder than the rest of them. For the first time since she turned eight, she felt the sweet relief of being completely honest with Tara and Ruby. And even though the magic ring gave Meg superpowers, Meg realized that the super-est things in her life were her best friends.

Sammy Griffin is a children's book author and super-geek who fangirls over superheroes and comic books in real life. She lives in Idaho Falls, Idaho, with her super-geek family.

Micah Player was born in Alaska and now lives in the mountains of Utah with a schoolteacher named Stephanie. They are the parents of two rad kids, one brash Yorkshire terrier, and several Casio keyboards.

micahplayer.com

Journey to some magical places and outer space, rock out, and soar among the clouds with these other chapter book series from Little Bee Books!

Isle of
MISFITS
FIRST CLASS

by JAMIE MAE   illustrated by FREYA HARTAS

——— chapter one ———

THE LONELIEST GARGOYLE

Gibbon the gargoyle lived atop the same castle all his life. Gargoyles were meant to protect the buildings they lived on. Sometimes, that meant protecting the people inside those buildings, too. That's what Gibbon was always taught.

But Gibbon couldn't stay still in one place *all* day. Sure, it was what he was *supposed* to do, but it was so boring! So Gibbon found something new to do to pass the time: playing pranks on people as they walked by below.

And winter was his favorite season for pranks. Winter meant snowballs.

One snowy day, he saw a man in a suit hurrying by the castle. Gibbon quickly made a snowball in his hands. He held it over the edge and dropped it, watching as it hit the man right on the head.

The man jumped from the shock of the cold snow. A confused look crossed his face when he didn't see anyone around.

Holding back laughter, Gibbon rolled another snowball and dropped it on the man. This time, the man yelped and ran off.

"*Gibbon!*" a voice whispered harshly.

He jumped and turned toward the gargoyle speaking to him. Elroy was the leader of the castle gargoyles and almost never broke his silence.

"That's enough," Elroy ordered. "You are too old to be playing pranks on the humans. You need to start taking your post seriously."

"But it's so boring!" Gibbon protested. "We just stand around all day. Even at night, we do nothing! Who are we even defending the castle from anyway?"

Elroy did not move, but his eyes glared over at Gibbon. "You need to learn how to work with your team, Gibbon. Your slacking off only makes it harder for the rest of us."

With a sigh, Gibbon looked down at the street. He watched as a group of kids stopped below the castle. One of them picked up some snow and threw it at another. Instead of getting mad, the other kid started laughing and made his own snowball. In no time at all, the kids were in a full-fledged snowball fight!

Maybe if I can get Elroy to play, everyone else will loosen up! he thought.

Gibbon smiled at Elroy. "Hey, catch me if you can! If you do, I'll be quiet and guard the castle the rest of the day!"

With a laugh, Gibbon took off. He climbed down the side of the castle, then darted down an empty street.

Gibbon knew—he just *knew*—if Elroy played with him, he'd understand.

But when he stopped and looked back, he didn't see Elroy. His heart sank.